Bringing Home Mr. Wrong

EMMA BRAY

CHAPTER

One

John

THE PARTY IS in full swing as I lean against the bar, whiskey in hand, trying to look interested in Frank's golf story for the dozenth time. My eyes wander the room and then I see *her*.

Camila.

My best friend's daughter, home from college for her dad's 50th.

She's radiant, her dark hair falling in soft waves, her lithe body moving gracefully through the crowd. It's been months since I've seen her, but something feels different this time. When her eyes meet mine across the room, I feel a jolt of electricity course through me.

I try to dismiss it, to remind myself she's far too young, that my feelings are wholly inappropriate. But I can't deny the spark between us, the way my heart pounds faster when she smiles in my direction. Shame burns through me as I recall the fantasies that fill my head late at night—her naked body against mine, her soft sighs and moans. I take a long swig of whiskey, welcoming the burn, trying to douse the desire smoldering inside me.

I try to ignore her presence, but that's like trying to ignore the sun. Camila is a like a shining light in a sea of darkness. My eyes are constantly drawn to her.

Those beautiful fucking curves.

My cock twitches in my pants as I keep glancing at her. My palms itch to trace over that beautiful dip in her waist, those perfect hips, her perky little breasts.

I imagine kissing my way down the column of her throat. I imagine how her skin would taste beneath my tongue—salty and sweet, like forbidden fruit. My fingers twitch, aching to tangle in her chestnut tresses, to tug her head back and expose the smooth expanse of her neck to my hungry mouth.

God, the things I want to do to her. The way I want to worship every inch of her nubile body, bringing her to the brink of ecstasy again and again until she's trembling and spent in my arms. I want to hear my name fall from her lips like a prayer as I bury myself deep inside her.

My gaze lingers on her pert ass as she glides through the room, the clingy fabric of her dress highlighting every tantalizing curve. I imagine grabbing those firm cheeks, squeezing the flesh as I grind my hardness against her. I picture bending her over the kitchen counter, bunching that tight little dress up around her waist, and sinking into her sweet, virgin depths from behind.

Fuck. I'm going straight to hell for the depraved things I want to do to my best friend's baby girl.

I down the rest of my whiskey in one gulp, relishing the fiery trail it blazes down my throat. The burn is a welcome distraction from the desire coursing through my veins, from the sinful images flooding my mind.

I set the empty glass on the bar with a heavy clink, my fingers tightening around it briefly as if the action could somehow ground me, could tether me to some semblance of reason or propriety. But it's futile. I'm already lost, drowning in a sea of forbidden longing, consumed by the kind of hunger that could destroy everything in a second.

Camila

The party is too loud. There are too many people I barely know gushing over how grown up I look now. I slip into the kitchen, needing a moment away from the chatter and laughter filling the house.

My skin feels flushed, though whether it's from the wine or from the intensity of John's gaze, I can't be sure. I open the fridge, letting the cool air wash over me as I reach for a bottle of water.

"Needed a break from the crowd?" His deep voice startles me and I spin around. John is leaning against the doorframe, his blue eyes boring into mine.

"Yeah, it's a bit overwhelming," I manage, my voice coming out breathier than I intend. He takes a step closer and I flush.

What is wrong with me? This is just John, my

dad's best friend. I've been around him my whole life. Why is his presence unsettling me so tonight?

"You know me, I've never been one for big parties," I say, trying to steady the tremor in my voice. He moves closer and leans against the counter, his presence both unnerving and thrilling.

"Your dad sure knows how to draw a crowd though. Guess that's expected for the big 5-0." His voice is low and smooth, his eyes never leaving mine. "You look beautiful, by the way. Hard to believe you're the same little girl who used to put on puppet shows in my living room."

My face grows hot at the compliment even as I laugh at the memory. "I haven't been a little girl for a long time," I whisper, holding his gaze. The air between us is charged, electric, and I'm acutely aware of every inch of my body.

His hand reaches out, brushing a stray lock of hair from my face, his fingers grazing my cheek. It's the barest of touches but it ignites something deep within me, a longing I've never felt before.

He agrees, something heated simmering beneath his gaze, "You're not a little girl anymore, that's for sure. Your dad mentioned you're doing really well at college too."

Pride swells in my chest, but it's overshadowed by the tension crackling in the scant space between us, the way John's eyes keep dropping to my lips. I know I shouldn't be so hyperaware of him, that he's my dad's best friend and twice my age. But I can't deny how badly I want to close the distance and press my mouth to his.

There's something about John. Truth be told, I've always had a little crush on him.

"I should go," he murmurs, but he makes no move to leave. We stand there, suspended in the moment, the distant laughter and music fading away until there is only the sound of our mingled breathing and the pounding of my heart.

Finally, he steps back, breaking the spell. "Goodnight, Camila," he says softly, before turning and disappearing down the hall.

I lean back against the cool metal of the fridge, my legs suddenly wobbly. I know I shouldn't want him, that it's wrong on so many levels.

I watch him go, unable to tear my eyes off his broad shoulders and trim waist. The man I've always looked up to as an uncle is now something else entirely—a tantalizing, forbidden desire I can't ignore any longer. I knew coming home would be a mistake. I just never thought it would be for this reason.

CHAPTER

Two

CAMILA

I stare at my phone, John's number glowing on the screen. My thumb hovers over the text button, heart pounding.

It's been two weeks since I returned to college, but I can't stop thinking about him—those piercing blue eyes, the way his strong hands felt on my cheek.

I take a deep breath and start typing.

Hey John, I was wondering if I could get your advice on something? I'm trying to decide what internships to apply for this summer and thought you might have some good insight, with all your experience. No pressure though! Hope you're doing well.

My finger shakes as I hit send. I feel a thrill and a pang of guilt all at once. Texting him like this, is it crossing a line? He's my dad's best friend...but there was a undeniable spark between us at Dad's birthday party. I can't just ignore it anymore.

Three dots appear. My heart races. Then his reply pops up:

Hi Camila, great to hear from you. I'd be happy to look over some options with you and share my thoughts. Why don't you send me a list of the ones you're considering? Hope your semester is off to a good start.

I grin, a flutter in my chest. His message is casual but warm. It's a start.

***

Over the next few days, we message back and forth about internships, but our texts gradually shift into more personal territory—updates on his latest projects, my classes and roommate dramas, jokes and memes. I find myself checking my phone obsessively, disappointed when there's no new notification from him.

One night, feeling bold from a little too much wine, I send a winking face emoji after a flirty quip. Heart pounding, I wait for his response.

The grey dots linger, disappear, then finally his reply:

Shouldn't you be focused on your studies instead of texting a boring old architect all night? ;)

Boring and old? Yeah right. I think of all the times I've caught him straight out of a run, t-shirt clinging to his toned chest. The way I've caught him looking at me over dinner when Dad wasn't paying attention...

Oh please, you're hardly boring OR old. But you're right, I should get some beauty rest. Sweet dreams John. Talk to you tomorrow :)

I put down the phone with a smile, mind racing

with possibilities. I know I'm playing with, fire but I can't seem to stop myself.

Rules are meant to be broken, right?

***

John

I frown at my phone, Camila's latest message lighting up the screen. That goodnight text with the little smile...she's flirting with me. Blatantly. And I'm flirting back like some lovesick teenager, when I should know better.

I run a hand over my face and sigh. This is Camila—Frank's daughter, the sweet little girl who used to sit on my shoulders and beg for piggyback rides.

But she's not a little girl anymore, is she? She's a beautiful, vivacious young woman. Full of passion and dreams and a light that draws me to her like a moth to a flame.

She's forbidden fruit. The age gap, my relationship with her father...I can list a million reasons why pursuing this is a terrible idea.

And yet, when she texts me, I can't help but respond.

I read over her message again, considering my reply. *Keep it light, John. Don't encourage her.*

But my fingers seem to move of their own accord as I type back:

Trust me, I think you're getting plenty of beauty rest. You look gorgeous as always. But I won't keep you up. Talk to you tomorrow, sweet dreams.

I hit send before I can second guess myself. Christ, I'm in trouble. This flirtation is dangerous and I know it. If Frank ever found out...I can't even imagine.

I should put a stop to this right now.

But when my phone pings with her response a minute later—a blushing smile and a heart—I feel a thrill shudder through me, and I know I won't.

I *can't.*

The temptation is simply too strong to resist.

I want her, consequences be damned.

I'm playing with fire too...and I have a feeling we're both about to get burned. Do I care?

I look at Camila's name on my screen and I know the answer is no. She's worth the risk.

***

One weekend, Camila convinces me to meet her for coffee when she's home on break from college. I walk into the cozy little shop, the scent of fresh brewed coffee and warm pastries greeting me as I enter. I spot her right away, her chestnut hair cascading over her shoulders like a silken curtain, drawing my gaze to her full lips, and I have to force myself not to stare. We exchange hellos, butterflies already taking flight in my stomach.

We take a seat in a quiet corner booth, our knees occasionally brushing under the table as we talk. Our conversation is light at first, but as the minutes tick by, it takes a decidedly flirtatious turn. I can't remember the last time I've felt this alive...this...*consumed*.

The air between us crackles with a palpable tension, so thick I could practically reach out and touch it. I'm acutely aware of every breath she takes, every flicker of those expressive hazel eyes that seem to hold a thousand secrets—secrets I'm desperate to unravel.

Camila's hand brushes against mine, sending a jolt of electricity straight to my core. She doesn't pull away. Instead, she laces our fingers together, her gaze questioning, a delicate blush creeping up her porcelain cheeks.

For a moment, sanity threatens to return, reminding me of the consequences we could face if anyone were to find out about this.

But I don't care and neither does she.

We continue to talk, and then we leave the coffee shop and walk through the park, both of us hesitant for this forbidden meeting to end.

When we finally come to a stop, I stare at her, and she stares back at me. Her lips part, as if they're inviting me in.

And God help me, but I can't say no.

I lean in, my heart pounding in my chest like a drummer on a feverish beat, and brush my lips against hers. Soft as a whisper, her lips part further, her tongue snaking out to meet mine, and I'm lost.

Our kiss deepens, my hand curling around her neck, angling her face upwards to deepen our connection. Her tongue dances with mine, as if she's been waiting for this moment as much as I have.

Finally, we both pull back, panting, our breaths mingling in the chill winter air. Our eyes meet, and I see the same heady mix of desire and trepidation mirrored in hers. We've crossed a line, and there's no going back now.

"We...we should probably...talk," she stutters, her voice thick with emotion.

I nod, my own voice unsteady. "S-sure."

We both know what we're about to embark on is nothing short of insanity. But as I stare into Camila's smoldering eyes, I know I'd walk through the fiery pits of hell and back for her.

And as we turn back to our respective cars, I vow to myself, I'll do everything in my power to keep this secret.

Our secret.

Forever.

CHAPTER
Three

CAMILA

The winter air bites my cheeks as I hurry across the deserted campus quad, my breath forming small clouds in the chilly darkness. I pull my coat tighter, but it's not just the cold making me shiver. It's the delicious thrill of anticipation, knowing I'll be in John's arms soon.

We've been stealing moments together for weeks now, sneaking off to quiet spots whenever I'm home from college. Quick coffee dates, walks in secluded parks, heated kisses in his car.

We have yet to go all the way yet, but every secret rendezvous only makes me fall harder. The way his eyes crinkle when he smiles just for me, how his hands skim my curves like he's memorizing every inch...

I reach the parking lot behind the library where he's waiting. His silver Audi gleams under the streetlights.

I tap on the window and slide into the warm leather seat beside him.

"Hey beautiful," John murmurs, his blue eyes drinking me in. "I missed you."

"I missed you too," I whisper back, my skin already tingling from his nearness. "Thanks for meeting me."

His fingers lace with mine over the console. "I'd meet you anytime, anywhere. You know that."

I lean in, breathing in his familiar scent of cedarwood and musk. Our lips meet, soft at first, then more urgently. A low moan escapes me as his tongue teases the seam of my mouth. God, the things this man does to me...

But even as I lose myself in his kiss, guilt niggles the back of my mind. My dad. His best friend. The secret we're keeping from him hangs between us.

I pull back reluctantly. "I hate lying to him, John. I don't know how much longer I can do this."

He exhales heavily, cupping my face with a rough palm. "I know, Camila. I don't like it either.

But we agreed to wait until you graduate to tell him. It's only a few more months."

"I know. I just...I love you so much. I don't want to hide it anymore."

I clap my hand over my mouth. I can't believe I just let that slip out like that. My face colors as I peek over at John for his reaction.

His eyes soften as he removes my hands from my face.

"I love you too, sweetheart. More than anything."

He kisses me so tenderly it almost breaks my heart, and then he rests his forehead against mine and I close my eyes, letting his words wash over me, soothing my troubled heart. For now, it's enough to be here in this moment. The future can wait.

***

John

I love you too, sweetheart. More than anything.

The words come straight from my soul and I rest my brow against hers, breathing her in. I know it's crazy. We haven't even had sex yet, but the words are true.

She's everything I never knew I needed. I'm

risking it all to be with her, but god help me, she's worth it.

"Let's get out of here," I murmur, reluctantly releasing her. "I know a place we can grab a bite to eat. Somewhere no one will see us."

Her smile is tremulous but trusting as she reaches for her seatbelt. "Lead the way."

I put the car in gear and point it towards the highway leading out of town. We have a few hours to make some memories before real life intrudes again. I plan to make every minute count.

Dinner is fantastic. Everything seems brighter in light of our confession.

The small Italian bistro is intimate and cozy, with flickering candles on the tables and the rich aroma of garlic and herbs in the air. I requested a private booth in the back, and as we slide in across from each other, our knees brush under the table, sending tingles up my thigh and straight to my dick.

Fuck, how I *want* her. Not just her beautiful body but *her*. Her heart. Her soul. I love everything about her.

We sip ruby red wine and share bites of pasta, talking and laughing quietly. But there's a new undercurrent between us now, an electric aware-ness that has me aching to be alone with her. I want to touch her, taste her, feel her skin against mine with no barriers between us.

After dinner, there's a palpable tension between us as I drive us back to my place. I reach over and place my hand on Camila's thigh, and I can feel her trembling.

My cock is a hard rod of steel in my pants, and it's taking everything in me not to blow my load right here just smelling the sweet scent of her perfume in my car.

When we finally reach my place, I help her out of the car and no sooner are we in the house than we're on each other. I crash my lips onto her, kissing her desperately, weeks of pent-up desire finally flooding forth.

"Fuck, Camila, baby, I want you so bad," I rasp against her lips as I hump her crudely through our clothes.

She moans into my mouth, her slim body writhing against mine as our tongues tangle urgently. "I want you too, John. So much," she pants, her hands fisting in my hair. "Please..."

I scoop her up, my hands cupping her perfect ass, and carry her to my bedroom. Moonlight spills across the bed as I lay her down on the charcoal sheets, drinking in the sight of her in my bed.

Where she fucking belongs, dammit.

Her chestnut hair is fanned out on the pillow. Her hazel eyes are dark with need. Her pink lips are parted and panting.

My beautiful girl.

I hover over her, my heart hammering as I take in every exquisite detail of her face. The slope of her nose, the arch of her brows, the sweet dip of her cupid's bow. I want to memorize it all, burn it into my brain.

"Are you sure about this, sweetheart?" I ask hoarsely, searching her eyes. "We can stop anytime. I don't want to rush you."

"I'm sure, John," she breathes, reaching up to stroke my face. "I want this. I want you."

Her words unleash something primal in me. I capture her lips in a searing kiss as my hands roam her lush curves, mapping her body through the thin fabric of her dress. She arches into my touch, little mewls of pleasure escaping her.

"Please," she whimpers when I trail my lips down the column of her throat. "Touch me..."

I work the zipper of her dress down with shaking fingers until the garment pools at her waist. My breath catches as I take in the sight of her in a nude lace bra, the dusky rose of her nipples visible through the sheer cups.

"Fucking beautiful," I groan, palming the heavy

swells of her breasts. "You're so perfect, Camila. I can't believe you're mine."

She flushes prettily and reaches behind to unclasp her bra. It falls away and I have to bite back a curse at the reveal of her bare tits, full and ripe and tipped with pebbled peaks just begging for my mouth.

I lower my head and take one rosy nipple between my lips, swirling my tongue around the bud before suckling greedily. Camila cries out sharply, her back bowing off the bed. I lavish the same attention on the other breast, my hand drifting down to slip beneath her dress and cup her through damp lace panties.

"Oh god," she pants, writhing against my palm as I rub slow circles over her clothed sex. "That feels so good..."

I hook my fingers in her panties and tug them down her legs, groaning when I see how wet she is, her folds glistening with arousal.

I *have* to taste her.

Easing down her body, I nudge her thighs apart and breathe in the heady scent of her before running my tongue along her slit.

"John!" she keens, her hips bucking wildly as I lick into her, savoring her tangy sweetness. I rapidly bring her to the edge with lips and tongue and fingers, sucking her swollen clit as I work two digits into her tight sheath.

She comes apart with a strangled scream, her inner muscles clenching greedily around my fingers as she rides out her climax.

I groan into her flesh, so fucking hard it hurts, desperate to be inside her. I work her through the aftershocks with soft licks and gentle caresses until she's limp and sated beneath me.

Crawling back up her body, I claim her mouth in a deep, drugging kiss, letting her taste herself on my tongue. She whimpers and clutches at my shoulders, our heavy breaths mingling.

"I need you, John," she rasps against my lips, her hips canting up to grind against my aching cock. "Please, I'm ready..."

I don't need any more encouragement. Shucking off my shirt and pants in record time, I settle between her splayed thighs, the broad head of my dick nudging insistently at her entrance.

"Look at me, sweetheart," I urge hoarsely, bracing my weight on my elbows. Her hazel eyes flutter open, hazy and dark with want, and lock onto mine. Emotion clogs my throat. "I love you so much. I need you to know that."

"I love you too," she whispers.

I cup her face in between my hands as I will her

to understand, "I'm fucking obsessed with you, Camila. Always have been. We do this…and there's no going back. You're going to be *mine*. Do you understand me, little girl?"

She bites her lip and nods. "Yes," she whispers. "I'm yours."

I stare into her eyes, and then I'm pushing into her, slowly, carefully, groaning at the exquisite feel of her tight heat enveloping me inch by throbbing inch.

"Oh god, John…" Camila gasps, her nails digging into my back, her body trembling as it stretches to accommodate my not insubstantial size.

Fucking hell! She feels so good. So tight. Mother*fuck*. I can't think. All I can do is stare into her eyes as I struggle to breath, the sensations of her virgin pussy overwhelming me.

I'm going to nut before I ever get fully inside her if I'm not careful.

I'm straining with the effort to hold back, every muscle in my body tight. I still when I'm fully sheathed, buried to the hilt in her slick warmth, giving her time to adjust. It's an exercise in restraint, everything in me screaming to take her hard and fast, but I won't hurt her.

"You feel so good," I grit out, my muscles quivering with the effort to hold back. "So perfect. Like you were made for me."

She makes a needy sound and rocks her hips, taking me even deeper. "Please, I need...I need..."

That's all the permission I need. I withdraw almost all the way before slamming back in, setting a slow, deep rhythm that has her keening.

The wet sounds of our bodies moving together mingle with our harsh pants and low moans. Moonlight bathes our writhing forms as I make love to her, pouring every ounce of my devotion into each roll of my hips.

"Do you know how many times I've imagined this?" I rasp. I'm delirous with pleasure, and all my dirty secrets come pouring out. "Do you know how hard it was watching you prance around in front of me in those little shorts you started wearing in high school? How many nights I had to come home and jack off to thoughts of my best friend's daughter? You were always fucking teasing me. So fucking innocent. Never even knew what you were doing to me. Keeping my cock hard for you all the time. Been needing to tear this pussy up for years."

"Ah, ah, ah, John," she chants with each powerful thrust, her head thrashing on the pillow. "More! More!"

I vary my angle slightly and she cries out as I

hit that spongy spot deep inside. Her legs come up to wrap around my waist, her heels digging into my ass as she urges me on.

Planting my knees, I rise up and grip her hips, pistoning into her harder and faster, chasing our pleasure. The headboard slams against the wall with each driving thrust as I pound into her sweet, tight cunt. Her pussy clenches around my cock like a velvet vise, gripping me so perfectly.

"Fuck, baby, I'm close," I grunt, my hips jack-hammering relentlessly, sweat dripping down my chest. "You gonna come for me? Gonna milk my cock with this greedy little pussy?"

"Yes, yes, oh god John, I'm gonna come!" Camila wails, her back arching off the bed as she digs her nails into my straining biceps.

I feel her start to flutter around my shaft and I reach between us to rub tight circles on her swollen clit. "That's it, sweetheart. Let go. Come all over my cock. Fucking drench me," I command gruffly.

She shatters with a keening cry, her cunt rippling and gushing around me as she comes hard. Her release triggers my own and I roar out my pleasure as I empty myself inside her with pulsing jets of cum.

"Fuck, Camila!" I groan, my hips churning erratically as I ride out the mind-blowing orgasm, filling her with my seed.

I collapse on top of her, both of us panting harshly, our sweat-slicked bodies trembling in the aftermath. I pepper her face with gentle kisses, brushing her damp hair back from her flushed cheeks.

"I love you," I rasp, my voice raw with emotion. "I love you so goddamn much."

"I love you too, John," she whispers back, her hazel eyes glowing up at me in the moonlight, so soft and trusting it makes my chest ache. "That was...incredible."

"You're incredible," I murmur, capturing her lips in a slow, deep kiss that leaves us both breathless.

I roll us to our sides, still joined intimately, and pull her back against my chest, spooning her smaller body with mine. My hand splays across her belly possessively as I nuzzle into the fragrant silk of her chestnut hair.

She sighs contentedly, lacing her fingers through mine over her stomach.

This is worth every risk, every sacrifice. *She's* my forever. Even if it means shattering the other most important bond in my life.

I'll break my best friend's heart to keep hers.

***

The next morning Camila lets me hold her for a long while before she finally breaks the silence.

"I want to bring you home for Christmas. As my date. Tell Dad about you."

I stiffen. "Camila, are you sure that's a good idea? Maybe we should—"

"No, John." She presses a finger to my lips, silencing me. "I'm done hiding. I love you, and I'm not ashamed of it. Besides, how mad can he be once he sees how happy we make each other?"

I want to believe that so bad it hurts. But I've known her father for too long, and the depth of his disapproval when it comes to his little girl is no secret. "Okay," I reluctantly agree, unable to stand against her determined expression. "We'll do it your way."

Her grin is reward enough, and for a fleeting moment, I allow myself to imagine a future where the three of us are a family—messy, unconventional, but full of love.

"I better get you back to college," I say as I reluctantly slip out of bed.

Camila pouts but doesn't argue. Instead, she pulls on my shirt, the one that carries her scent and presses a lingering kiss to my lips. "I love you, John Hawkins."

"I love you too, Camila Winters."

I hold her in my arms one last time before gently setting her away from me. "I'll meet you at your father's for the Christmas party."

"You better be there, mister," she teases, but there's a hint of vulnerability in her eyes. "I'll have my dad's favorite whiskey ready, just the way you taught me."

"Well, then how can I say no?" I murmur, planting one last kiss on her forehead before grabbing my coat.

As I drop her back off at college, the wintery New York City skyline twinkling in my rearview mirror, I feel a surge of determination. I'll do whatever it takes to make this work—even if it means facing her dad's wrath head-on. After all, nothing—not age, not distance, not even her overprotective father—is going to keep me from the woman I love.

Four

JOHN

I step into the festively decorated foyer, breathing in the scent of cinnamon and pine. My heart races as Camila emerges from the living room, her chestnut hair cascading over the shoulders of her emerald dress that hugs her petite frame. Her hazel eyes meet mine, sparkling with a mix of joy and trepidation.

Before we can exchange more than a tentative smile, her father bounds over, beaming. "John, my old friend! So glad you could make it." He claps me on the back.

I plaster on a grin, trying to ignore the guilt twisting in my gut as I glance between him and

Camila. "Wouldn't miss it, Frank. Thanks for having me."

Camila opens her mouth to speak, but Frank ushers us into the dining room. "Come, come, dinner's about to be served!"

As everyone takes their seats around the long oak table, I slip into the chair beside Camila. She leans in close, her jasmine perfume enveloping me. "We'll find a moment to tell him...together," she whispers, resting a hand on my knee under the table.

I nod subtly, covering her hand with mine. Even that simple touch sends electricity arcing through my veins. "Of course. Let's just get through dinner first."

Relaxed chatter fills the room as Frank carves the turkey, but every nerve in my body is attuned to Camila's presence at my side. I'm hyperaware of each brush of her arm, every knowing look from beneath her long lashes. The secret of our forbidden romance hangs heavily between us, a delicious tension ready to snap.

As dishes are passed, my fingers graze Camila's, lingering a moment too long. Frank raises an eyebrow at me from across the table. I quickly look away, focusing intently on scooping mashed potatoes onto my plate.

"John, I meant to say, it means the world to have you here." Frank's voice cuts through the din of clattering silverware. "Lord knows you've been like a brother to me all these years. I couldn't ask for a better man to have my back."

His words twist the knife of betrayal deeper into my chest. I meet his earnest gaze, forcing a smile. "I'm honored, Frank. Your friendship has always meant a lot to me too."

Camila squeezes my knee reassuringly. I chance a look at her and the tenderness shimmering in her eyes momentarily calms the storm inside me. Beneath the table, hidden from view, I lace my fingers through hers.

Her touch grounds me, even as my heart wages war with my head. I know every stolen glance, every secret caress only compounds my dishonesty. But damn me to hell, I cannot deny the way this brilliant, passionate woman has utterly bewitched me, body and soul.

Conversation continues to flow around us, but Camila and I are lost in our own world. With every passing minute, the need to confess the depths of our feelings grows, a living thing pulsing between us.

I only hope that when the truth finally comes to light, the strength of our love will weather the storm of a father's fury and a friend's crushing disappointment.

***

Later that night, I pace the hardwood floors of my dimly lit living room, a tumbler of whiskey in hand. The warm amber glow of the lamp casts long shadows across the room, as tortured as my own thoughts.

A soft knock at the door makes my pulse leap. I set down my drink and cross the room in a few swift strides, easing open the door. Camila slips inside, snowflakes clinging to her hair like a crown of crystals. In the low light, her eyes glimmer with a mix of longing and uncertainty that mirrors my own.

"John," she breathes, stepping into my arms. I enfold her in my embrace, savoring the way her curves melt against me, her face buried in the crook of my neck. For a moment, the world falls away and there is only her—the heat of her body, the intoxicating scent of her hair, the drum of her heartbeat against my chest.

I tilt her chin up and capture her lips in a searing kiss, pouring all my pent-up desire into the crush of my mouth on hers. She responds with equal fervor, her fingers raking through my hair, nails grazing my scalp.

A groan escapes me as I walk her backward, never breaking the kiss, until her back meets the wall. My hands skim over her sides, her hips, hungry to map every dip and swell I've been aching to touch all evening.

She breaks away with a gasp. "John, wait..."

I pull back slightly, my chest heaving. "What's wrong?"

Camila bites her kiss-swollen lip. "I've been thinking. Maybe...maybe we should wait to tell Dad. Until after the holidays."

An icy tendril of dread curls in my stomach. I search her face for clues, trying to decipher the hesitation in her eyes. "Camila, I thought you wanted this. To stop hiding. To finally be together, openly and honestly."

She cups my face in her delicate hands. "I do, John. More than anything. But I saw how happy Dad was tonight, having us all together under one roof. I don't want to ruin Christmas for him."

I exhale heavily, pulling away to rake a hand through my hair. "And after? What then? We just go back to sneaking around, lying to everyone we care about?"

Hurt flashes across her features and I instantly regret my harsh tone. "No, of course not," she says softly. "But a few more days...is that so much to ask? To give us time to find the right words?"

I turn to stare out the frost-limned window, jaw clenched. The city sparkles beyond the glass like a thousand fallen stars, cold and distant. Camila's reflection appears beside mine, her brow creased with worry.

"John, please. I'm not having second thoughts."

Camila's fingers brush the small of my back as she steps closer, her warmth radiating through my shirt. "I could never doubt this, doubt us. But I need to do this the right way. Can you understand that?" Her voice is barely a whisper, threaded with raw emotion.

I turn to face her, the ache in my chest eclipsing the anger simmering in my veins. Her eyes shine with unshed tears, vulnerability etched into every line of her beloved face. I reach out to trace the delicate curve of her cheekbone. "I do understand. It's just...I'm tired of pretending, Camila. Of acting like you don't mean everything to me."

She leans into my touch, her lips grazing my palm. "I know. God, John, every second we're apart feels like an eternity. Having you so close tonight, but not being able to really be with you...it's torture." A single tear slips free, trailing a glistening path down her cheek.

I catch the salty drop with my thumb, gently wiping it away. "Shh, sweetheart. I'm sorry. I didn't mean to push. I just love you so damn much." The words catch in my throat, rough with feeling.

Camila rises up on her toes, her mouth finding mine in a gentle, yielding kiss. I pour every ounce of devotion into the careful slide of my lips over hers, memorizing the plush give of her flesh, the honeyed taste of her tongue.

She melts into me, fingers twisting in the fabric of my shirt. I walk us backwards until my calves hit the sofa. Sinking down onto the cushions, I gather her into my lap, never breaking the drugging kiss. She straddles my hips, the hem of her dress riding up to reveal the creamy expanse of her thighs.

I run my palms reverently over the exposed skin, relishing the way her breath hitches as I graze the lace edge of her panties. She rocks subtly against me, kindling a fire low in my belly. I nip at her bottom lip, soothing the sting with a languid lick.

"I love you too, John. So much it terrifies me." The hushed words ghost across my cheek as she trails open-mouthed kisses along my jaw, down the column of my throat. "I promise, as soon as Christmas is over, we'll sit down with Dad. Come clean about everything."

I hum in agreement, tilting my head back to give her better access. She laves her tongue over my pulse point and I shudder, my grip tightening on her hips. "And then," I rasp, fighting for coherence as she grinds sinuously against my hardening cock, "no more hiding. No more secrets."

"No more secrets," she echoes, her fingers deftly working open the buttons of my shirt. She pushes the fabric aside, exposing my heated skin to the cool air. Her lips blaze a trail down my chest as her hips rock maddeningly against mine, stoking the flames of my desire.

"Camila," I groan, my voice strained. "If you keep that up, I won't be able to control myself."

She lifts her head, eyes dark with want, a wicked smile playing at the corners of her kiss-bruised mouth. "Maybe I don't want you to control yourself." Her husky words send a jolt of pure, carnal need straight to my core.

With a low growl, I surge forward, capturing her mouth in a fierce, demanding kiss. I tangle one hand in her silken hair, the other splaying across the small of her back to crush her body flush against mine. She whimpers into the kiss, her fingers digging into my shoulders.

I strip her of her dress with urgent, fumbling hands, desperate to feel every inch of her. She shivers as the cool air kisses her fevered skin, clad now only in scraps of emerald lace. My hungry gaze rakes over her, drinking in the sight I've been starving for all night.

"You are so beautiful," I breathe, reverence and desire warring in my tone. I skim my fingers up her ribcage to cup the weight of her breasts, feeling her nipples pebble against my palms through the delicate fabric.

Camila arches into my touch with a breathy moan, her head falling back in abandon. I take advantage, ducking my head to press hot, open-mouthed kisses to the column of her throat. She writhes in my lap, seeking friction, and I oblige, thrusting my cloth-covered erection against her damp heat.

"Please, John," she keens, her nails scoring my back. "I need you."

Those words, raw and aching, shred the last of my restraint. I stand abruptly, lifting her with me. She locks her legs around my waist as I navigate us blindly to the bedroom, our lips locked in a messy, desperate tangle.

I lay her down on the bed like an offering, stepping back to shed my clothes with haste. She watches me through heavy-lidded eyes, her tongue darting out to wet her lips. Once divested, I crawl up her body, trailing worshipful kisses along her quivering stomach, the valley between her breasts, the delicate line of her collarbone.

"I love you," I murmur into her skin, a prayer and a promise. "No matter what happens, that will never change."

Tears glimmer in Camila's eyes as she pulls me down into a searing, soul-deep kiss. And as I finally sink into her welcoming heat, our bodies moving as one, I know that this—right here, right now—is worth fighting for. Worth weathering any storm, enduring any trial. Because a love like this, so raw and real it steals the breath from my lungs and sets my very soul ablaze, is the kind of love that only comes along once in a lifetime. If even that.

As our bodies move in perfect sync, skin sliding against sweat-slicked skin, breathy moans and whispered adorations filling the air, I lose myself in her. In this moment. This connection, profound and unbreakable.

Her silken heat grips me like a vice as I plunge into her depths, and I know I will never have my fill of her. Of this. Our rhythm builds, faster, harder, more urgent, rushing toward that precipice of ecstasy. Camila throws her head back with a keening cry, her inner muscles fluttering around my length as she comes undone beneath me.

I follow her over the edge with a guttural groan, burying my face in the crook of her neck as wave after wave of pleasure crashes over me, threatening to pull me under. I spill myself inside her, marking her, claiming her as mine in the most primal way.

As the aftershocks fade, I gather her trembling body close, pressing tender kisses to her damp brow, her eyelids, the tip of her nose. She curls into me with a contented sigh, fitting her curves to my angles as if we were made for each other. Perhaps we were.

"I love you," she murmurs drowsily, her fingers idly tracing patterns on my sweat-cooled chest. "No matter what happens when we tell my dad, that won't change. You're my forever, John Hawkins."

Emotion swells in my chest, so acute it borders on pain. I tilt her chin up to meet her heavy-lidded gaze, my thumb caressing the apple of her cheek. "Forever," I echo solemnly. "I promise you, Camila, I will never stop fighting for us. For this love. Come what may."

She seals that vow with a soft, lingering kiss. We drift off tangled together, content in our bubble of blissful afterglow. But even as slumber claims me, a niggling unease persists. The knowledge that reality awaits us come morning, cold and unforgiving.

Lying to Frank, even by omission, eats at me like a cancer. This man who is like a brother to me, who trusts me implicitly. Am I not betraying that sacred bond with every forbidden touch, every passionate embrace? The weight of my deceit threatens to crush me.

But as I look down at Camila, her face relaxed in sleep, dark lashes fanning over porcelain cheeks, kiss-swollen lips curved in a secret smile, I know I could never give her up. Not even for my best friend.

CHAPTER
Five

CAMILA

The delicate scent of gingerbread and pine fills the air as I descend the stairs, my heart fluttering like the lights on the tree. John stands by the fireplace, his gaze meeting mine with an intensity that sends shivers down my spine. The distance between us feels electric, yet uncrossable.

"Merry Christmas, Camila," he says, his voice low and warm like honey.

"Merry Christmas," I manage, my words nearly catching in my throat. I ache to go to him, to lose myself in his embrace, but Dad's footsteps behind me tether me in place.

"Camila, can I talk to you for a sec?" Dad asks, his brow furrowed with concern.

Reluctantly, I tear my eyes from John and follow Dad into the kitchen. He studies me, his expression a mix of confusion and worry.

"Is everything okay, sweetie? You seem...distracted lately."

"I'm fine, Dad. Just stressed about school, that's all." The lie tastes bitter on my tongue. I hate deceiving him, but the truth is too terrifying to voice.

Dad nods slowly, unconvinced. "You know you can always talk to me, right? About anything."

"I know. Thanks, Dad." I force a smile, guilt twisting like a knife in my gut.

As Dad leaves to check on the turkey, John appears in the doorway, his presence filling the room. He steps closer, his fingertips grazing my arm, igniting a fire beneath my skin.

"Come over later," he whispers, his breath warm against my ear. "I have something for you."

I nod, yearning and apprehension warring within me. This secret is becoming too heavy to bear, but the thought of losing John is unbearable.

Hours later, I find myself on John's doorstep, my heart in my throat. He welcomes me inside, the house aglow with soft light and unspoken promises.

We settle on the couch, thighs brushing, the air between us thick with longing. John reaches beneath the tree and retrieves a small, wrapped box.

"Open it," he urges gently, eyes shimmering with emotion.

With trembling fingers, I tear away the paper to reveal a delicate silver locket. Inside, a tiny sketch of us together, rendered in exquisite detail.

"It's beautiful," I whisper, tears pricking my eyes. "I love it."

"And I love you," John murmurs, tucking a strand of hair behind my ear. "More than I ever thought possible."

I lean into his touch, my heart swelling with certainty.

"I'm ready," I breathe, my forehead resting against his. "I want to tell my dad about us. I don't want to hide anymore."

John's eyes search mine, a mixture of hope and hesitation swirling in their depths. "Are you sure, Camila? I don't want you to do anything you're not ready for."

"I've never been more sure of anything," I say, my voice steady despite the nerves fluttering in my stomach. "You're what I want, John. You're my future."

A slow smile spreads across John's face, his hand cupping my cheek with infinite tenderness. "You're my everything," he whispers, his lips brushing against mine.

The kiss starts soft and sweet, a gentle exploration of love long denied. But as John's arms tighten around me, the heat between us ignites into a fiery blaze. I melt into him, my fingers tangling in his hair, pulling him closer still. The locket dangles between us, a symbol of our unbreakable bond.

John lowers me onto the couch, his body covering mine, our limbs intertwined like vines seeking sunlight. His mouth trails scorching kisses down my neck as his hands skim over my curves, leaving goosebumps in their wake. I arch into his touch, a breathy moan escaping my lips.

Lost in a haze of sensation, we almost don't hear the sound of the front door opening. But the sharp intake of breath that follows snaps us back to reality with dizzying speed.

"What the hell is going on here?" My father's voice cracks like a whip, fury and disbelief etched into every line of his face.

John and I spring apart, but it's too late. The

damning evidence of our passion is written plainly across our swollen lips and rumpled clothing.

"Dad, I can explain," I begin, my voice shaking as I rise on unsteady feet.

"Explain? Explain how my daughter is wrapped around my best friend on his couch? How long has this been going on?" Dad demands, his face mottled red with anger.

John stands beside me, his hand finding mine, anchoring me. "Frank, please, just let us—"

"No!" Dad cuts him off. "I trusted you, John. I trusted you with my little girl, and this is how you repay me?"

"It's not like that," I protest, tears stinging my eyes. "We didn't plan this, it just...happened. But it's real, Dad. I love him."

Dad reels back as if I've slapped him, pain and betrayal flickering across his features. "Love? You're just a child, Camila. You don't know what love is."

"I'm not a child anymore," I say softly, my heart breaking at the hurt in his eyes. "And I do know what love is."

I move closer to John, reaffirming my stance as I square my shoulders. "I'm an adult, Dad, and you can't stop me. I'm going to be with John."

My dad turns his angry gaze to John. "Over my dead body."

Uh-oh.

CHAPTER
Six

JOHN

The world seems to tilt on its axis as Frank's words reverberate through the room, each syllable laced with accusation and disappointment. My heart clenches at the anguish in Camila's eyes, her hand trembling in mine as she faces her father's wrath.

"Frank, please," I try again, my voice rough with emotion. "Just let us explain. This isn't some fleeting fling. Camila and I... we have something real."

Frank's eyes flash dangerously, his hands balling into fists at his sides. "Real? You're twice her age, John! She's barely out of high school, for God's sake. How could you take advantage of her like this?"

"He didn't take advantage of me!" Camila cries out, stepping forward, her chin lifted defiantly even as tears streak down her face. "I'm an adult, Dad. I made my own choices. I chose John, and I'll keep choosing him, no matter what you say."

Pride and love swell in my chest at her fierce declaration, but it's tempered by the gutting realization of how deeply we've hurt Frank. This man who's been like a brother to me, who trusted me with his only daughter. I never meant for it to happen this way.

"Camila, sweetheart, maybe you should let your dad and I talk privately for a minute," I suggest gently, giving her hand a reassuring squeeze.

She looks at me uncertainly, her hazel eyes swimming with a tempest of emotions. After a long moment, she nods, pressing a soft kiss to my cheek before slipping out of the room. The skin tingles where her lips touched, a bittersweet reminder of all we stand to lose.

Frank watches her go, his expression unreadable. The silence stretches between us, taut and suffocating. Finally, he speaks, his voice low and eerily calm.

"How long, John?"

I swallow hard, meeting his gaze unflinchingly. "A few months. But my feelings for her...they've been growing for longer than that. I tried to fight it, Frank. I didn't want to betray your trust. But I couldn't deny what was in my heart."

Frank laughs, a harsh, mirthless sound. "Spare me the romance novel crap. You should have walked away the second you realized you had feelings for her. She's barely more than a kid, John. She doesn't know what she wants."

"With all due respect, I think you're underestimating her," I counter, an edge creeping into my voice. "Camila is smart, and strong, and capable of making her own decisions. What we have...it's not some teenage crush or a midlife crisis. It's real, and it's worth fighting for."

Frank shakes his head, a vein throbbing in his temple. "I can't believe what I'm hearing. After everything we've been through together, John. The years of friendship, the shared memories...and this is how you repay me? By seducing my daughter behind my back?"

The accusation cuts deep, twisting like a knife in my gut. "That's not how it was, Frank. I would never intentionally hurt you or Camila. But I can't change the way I feel about her."

"Well, you'd better start trying," Frank growls,

jabbing a finger at me. "Because if you think I'm going to stand by and watch you ruin my daughter's life, you've got another thing coming."

"Ruin her life?" I echo incredulously. "Frank, I love Camila. I want to build a future with her, not destroy her future."

"And what kind of future do you think you can offer her?" Frank demands, his face mottled with rage. "You're old enough to be her father, for Christ's sake! She deserves someone her own age, someone who can grow with her, not some washed-up old bachelor chasing after a younger woman."

Each word lands like a physical blow, and I flinch despite myself. "You don't mean that, Frank. You're upset, and I get it. But don't take this out on Camila. She doesn't deserve your anger."

"Oh, I'm just getting started with her," Frank seethes. "She's going to learn that actions have consequences. It's me or you."

Panic claws at my throat, desperation bleeding into my voice. "Frank, please. Don't do this. Camila needs you. We both do."

But Frank is already turning away, his shoulders rigid with barely contained fury. "You have until the end of the week to end things with her,

John. Or I swear to God, I'll make sure you never see her again."

With that, he storms out, slamming the door behind him with enough force to rattle the windows. I sink onto the couch, burying my face in my hands as the weight of his ultimatum crashes over me.

Lose Camila, or lose Frank.

How am I supposed to choose between the woman I love and the man who's been like a brother to me? The thought of a life without Camila at my side is unbearable, a yawning chasm of emptiness and regret.

But the prospect of losing Frank's friendship, of fracturing the bond we've shared for decades...it's equally devastating. He's been a constant in my life for as long as I can remember, the one person I could always count on, no matter what.

But I already know I'll choose Camila. I'd choose her a thousand times over. She's my heart and soul.

I'm not a crying man, but now I let the tears come, my shoulders shaking with silent sobs as the enormity of the situation sinks in. Outside, the winter wind howls mournfully, a haunting echo of the turmoil raging in my heart.

CHAPTER
Seven

CAMILA

The silence in John's house is suffocating. I sit on the leather sofa, the coolness of it a sharp contrast to the heat rising in my cheeks. John paces the room, his brow furrowed with worry. The weight of our actions hangs heavy between us.

"He won't even speak to me," I whisper, my voice trembling. "My own father..."

John stops pacing and kneels before me, taking my hands in his. His touch is warm, comforting. "Give him time, Camila. This is a shock for him. For everyone."

I search his blue eyes, usually so calm and reassuring. Now they betray hints of uncertainty. "What if he never accepts us, John? What if we've ruined everything?"

He cups my face gently, his thumb brushing away a stray tear. "We'll find a way through this, together. I'm not giving up on us, Camila. On you."

I lean into his touch, drawing strength from his steadfast presence. The spicy scent of his cologne envelops me like a protective cocoon. But doubt still gnaws at the edges of my mind, persistent and relentless. Can our love weather this storm? Is it strong enough to mend the fractures we've caused?

Days bleed into each other, the tension never abating. Dad's silence is a wall between us, impenetrable and unyielding. Each unanswered call, each ignored text, is a dagger to my heart. I cling to John, my anchor in this turbulent sea of emotions. But even his reassurances begin to feel hollow, worn thin by the passage of time.

Finally, a glimmer of hope. Dad agrees to meet me, to talk. I sit across from him at our favorite café, the one where we've shared countless heart-to-hearts over the years. The familiar aroma of coffee and baked goods does little to ease the tightness in my chest.

"Dad, please try to understand," I begin, my hands wrapped around my mug, seeking its warmth. "John is everything you've always wanted for me. He's smart, successful, responsible. It's not like he's some deadbeat. And you've been friends with him for so long, you know he's a good guy who would never hurt me. And more importantly, John makes me happy. Truly happy. Isn't that what you've always wanted for me?"

He sighs deeply, lines of hurt etched into his face. "I want you to be happy, Camila. But this... it's not right. He's too old for you, he's my best friend. How can I accept this?"

"Age is just a number, Dad. It's about how we feel, the connection we share. John is kind, supportive, and loves me for who I am. Can't you see that?"

I reach across the table, tentatively resting my hand on his. He doesn't pull away, and I take it as a small victory. "I know this is hard for you. But please, don't make me choose between the two most important men in my life. I need you both."

Silence stretches between us, heavy with unspoken emotions. Finally, Dad's shoulders slump, the fight draining out of him. "I can't pretend to be okay with this overnight, Camila. But...I'll try. For you."

Tears sting my eyes as relief floods through me. It's not a complete acceptance, but it's a start. A fragile bridge across the chasm that divides us. I squeeze his hand, pouring all my love and grati-tude into that simple gesture.

As I leave the café, the sun breaks through the clouds, casting a warm glow on the street. A symbol of hope, of new beginnings. The road ahead may be rocky, but with John by my side and Dad's tentative understanding, I know we'll find our way.

We have to.

CHAPTER
Eight

JOHN

I stand outside the familiar door, heart pounding in my chest. My fingers tighten around the bottle of scotch—a peace offering, perhaps. Or liquid courage. Drawing a deep breath, I knock.

The door opens, revealing the stoic face of my oldest friend. His eyes, once warm, now regard me with a cold distance. "John."

"Hi Frank, I was hoping we could talk." I hold up the bottle. "I brought your favorite."

He hesitates before stepping aside. "Come in."

The house feels different now, weighted with unspoken words and broken trust. We settle into armchairs, glasses in hand. The scotch burns my throat.

"I know you're angry," I begin, choosing each word carefully. "And you have every right to be. But I need you to know...my feelings for Camila are genuine. I would never do anything to hurt her."

His jaw clenches. "She's my little girl, John. I trusted you."

"I didn't plan this. It just...happened." Even to my own ears, it sounds weak. "I care for her, deeply."

Silence stretches between us, thick and suffocating. Finally, he sighs. "I don't like it. But...I can see she cares for you too." He meets my gaze, eyes fierce. "If you break her heart, we're done. Understand?"

I nod solemnly. "I promise, I'll do right by her. Always."

He drains his glass and stands. "I'll hold you to that."

Relief floods me as I rise, offering my hand. After a moment, he shakes it—a fragile truce. There's still a long road ahead, I know. But it's a start.

***

Camila

. . .

Twinkling lights and elegant garlands adorn every surface of my childhood home. The annual New Year's Eve party—a family tradition. But this year, everything's different.

I smooth my dress, scanning the crowded room. When my eyes find John, my heart flutters. He looks devastatingly handsome in his suit, with his dark hair and thick beard. Our gazes lock and he smiles, making his way towards me.

"You look beautiful," he murmurs, pressing a chaste kiss to my cheek. I blush, leaning into him.

"And you look handsome as ever." I take his hand, lacing our fingers.

We mingle, never straying far from each other. I catch my father watching us, his expression unreadable. But as the night wears on, I see the tension in his shoulders ease slightly.

"I think he's coming around," John whispers conspiratorially. "Slowly but surely."

I nod, hope blooming in my chest. It will take time—rebuilding the trust, finding a new normal. But I know that John and I can get through anything.

The countdown begins, voices rising in excited unison. John pulls me close, his eyes reflecting the shimmering lights. In this moment, I feel invincible.

And then the countdown begins.

"3...2...1! Happy New Year!" Cheers erupt all around us as confetti rains down, but John and I only have eyes for each other. The rest of the world falls away.

He cups my face tenderly, thumb grazing my cheekbone. "Happy New Year, Camila," he breathes, his voice low and intimate. "I love you, more than words can say."

"I love you too, John. So much." Emotion swells in my chest, threatening to overflow.

Slowly, reverently, he lowers his head. His lips brush against mine, soft and sweet at first, then deepening with unspoken promises. I sink into his embrace, savoring his familiar scent of sandalwood and spice. His strong arms anchor me, making me feel cherished. Protected.

When we finally part, I'm breathless and glowing, giddy bubbles of joy fizzing through my veins. John rests his forehead against mine, his eyes glittering with barely restrained desire. "To us," he toasts, his voice husky.

"To us," I echo.

My eyes lift, and I catch my father watching us across the room. He gives me a wordless nod. I guess it's as close to approval as I'm going to get it, so I'll gladly take it.

I smile up at John, my heart light. No more hiding, no more doubt. Just an unshakable certainty that this—that *he*—is exactly where I'm meant to be.

John claims my lips again, and I melt into his kiss, pouring every ounce of my love, my hopes, my dreams into this perfect midnight moment. A beautiful start to the rest of our lives.

Epilogue

Two years later

John

I WATCH Camila from across the room, my heart pounding with desire. Two years together and she still takes my breath away. Her chestnut hair cascades over her shoulders as she laughs, the sound musical and free. I imagine that laugh turning into moans of pleasure beneath me.

I cross to her, sliding an arm around her waist. "You're so beautiful," I murmur, nuzzling her neck. "I want you. Now."

She shivers and leans into me. "Oh John. I want you too. Always."

We tumble onto the bed, a tangle of limbs and heated skin. I explore the curves and valleys of her body, already so familiar yet always new and exciting. Camila arches under my touch, her hazel eyes burning into mine.

"I need you," she pants. "Please, John."

I position myself over her, nearly shaking with the intensity of my need. More than just physical, it's a bone-deep yearning, a primal urge. The desire to claim her, possess her. To plant my seed deep inside and watch it grow.

"I'm going to fill you up," I growl. "Put my baby in your belly."

Camila cries out as I surge forward, taking her in one hard thrust. Her nails rake my back as her legs wrap around me.

I piston my cock in and out of her for several strokes before she stops me with a hand to my chest.

I look down at her questioningly, hoping I haven't hurt her, but she slips out from underneath me and falls to her knees at the edge of the bed, looking up at me coyly from underneath her thick lashes.

Hell yes.

My girl takes my cock in her hands and licks her lips before her hot mouth engulfs me.

I groan as Camila's lips wrap around my shaft, her tongue swirling and teasing. The wet heat of her mouth is exquisite torture. She takes me deep, sucking hard, her hazel eyes locked on mine. I tangle my fingers in her silky hair, fighting the urge to thrust into her throat.

She works me to the brink with long, slow pulls, then releases me with an obscene pop. "I want your cum inside me, John," she purrs. "I want to carry our child."

A primal growl rips from my chest. In one swift motion, I yank her up and toss her on the bed. She lands with a little yelp that turns into a moan as I cover her body with mine.

I rub the swollen head of my cock through her slick folds, coating myself in her arousal. She's dripping wet, ready for me. Camila whimpers and lifts her hips, desperate for more.

"Fuck, look at you, you perfect little thing," I rasp. "You love sucking your man's cock, don't you, honey? It got you dripping wet, sweetheart."

"Please, John," she begs. "Give me your baby."

That shreds any ounce of self-control I had left.

I slam into her, burying myself to the hilt in her tight heat. She cries out, back bowing off the bed. I set a hard, deep rhythm, each powerful thrust hitting that perfect spot that makes her keen.

"You want me to breed this fertile little cunt?" I rasp in her ear. "Pump you full of my seed until it takes?"

"Yes, yes!" she sobs, nails scoring my shoulders. "Knock me up, John. I'm yours, all yours."

Her dirty pleas make my balls tighten, pushing me closer to the edge. Knowing she craves my child in her belly as much as I crave putting it there sends me into a frenzy. I pound into her, the obscene slap of flesh filling the room.

Camila meets me thrust for thrust, grinding her hips to take me impossibly deeper. "I'm close," she pants. "Come with me, John. Fill me up!"

Her walls clench around my cock as she shatters, milking me. With a roar, I bury myself one last time and explode, painting her insides with jet after jet of hot cum.

I collapse over her, both of us gulping for air. I press tender kisses to her face as I stay pressed deep inside her, reluctant to pull out.

"I love you," I tell her, voice gravelly with emotion.

"I love you too, John. So much."

We drift off, still joined, dreaming of our future growing in her womb.

Welcome to Bringing Home Trouble!
You can't choose who you fall in love with.

However, you can stir the pot or bring it to a rolling boil. Especially when your Bringing Home Trouble for the holidays. You'll love the swoon worthy heroes and their sweet heroine's. As they navigate the delicate balance of true love and family drama. Come along for the fun, as fourteen of your favorite insta-love authors tame the holidays with lots of steamy moments and find love. Check out the entire series here!

One Twisted Christmas ~ By Cassi Hart
My Ex's Dad is Coming To Town ~ By Eve London
Unwrapping His Naughty Secret ~ By Chloe Maine
Holidays and Handcuffs ~ By Natasha Sterling
Holiday Flame ~ By Kate Tilney
Gone Away Home ~ By Ember Davis
Tangled With The Professor ~ By Lizzy West
Big Nick Energy ~ By Mayra Statham
Bringing Home Mr. Wrong ~ By Emma Bray
A Christmas Collin ~ By Lena Little
Bringing Home The Bad Boy ~ By Jailaa West
Riding Dirty For Christmas ~ By Fern Fraser
Bringing Home The Biker ~ By Winter Travers

Christmas With The Convict ~ By Raven Moon

Want a free book from Emma Bray? Go to www.
authoremmabray.com.

Keep reading for an excerpt from Santa's Obsession.

Jenny

"Oh my god, just go!" Eve scrunches up her pale, little nose as she tries to keep a straight face. I've been badgering my bestie with all sorts of questions about the hunk I dared her to kiss at the Halloween party a few months ago. He just so happened to be her new boss, but it took them a while to figure out who the other was because they'd both been masked at the masquerade. Theirs was like a super smexy fairytale story complete with the happy ending. They ended up getting married, and I'm truly happy for my best friend. If anyone deserves happiness, it's my dark-haired little friend Eve who was born on Halloween.

But I won't lie to myself and say that I'm not insanely jealous of her because I am. I've seen the way Eve's husband showers her with attention. He has eyes for no one but her, and I'm not stupid. I know guys like to look at me. I get hit on all the time, and I'm a shameless flirt, but it's all a front.

Despite all my talk, I'm still a virgin. I've just never found someone who makes me all gooey inside the way Lucian obviously does Eve.

I feel like a bit of a prude to be twenty-one and still a virgin. Maybe that's why I put on such a show with all my flirting—to hide the fact that I'm about as inexperienced as they come. All I've ever done is kiss. None of my friends would ever believe me if I told them I'd never gone all the way.

I just never could bring myself to give it up to some loser who I didn't feel anything for, though.

Maybe I'm too spoiled or too much of a romantic at heart, but I want fireworks. I want unbridled passion and to know that he's *the one* before I commit my body to someone.

Is that too much to ask?

"Jenny," Eve's amused voice breaks me from my reverie as she points out, "you're going to be late."

I glance down at my phone and jump up with a curse, "Shit! I gotta go! Love ya, girl!"

I give Eve an air kiss before I jump in my hot pink car. It was an early birthday slash Christmas present from my parents.

Yes, I love pink, and yes, I'm a Christmas baby. In the autumn, I'm an unapologetically pumpkin-spice loving, scarf and boot-wearing white girl. So, shoot me. I'm a walking cliche, but I don't care. I'm just me.

Whereas my bestie might have been born on All Hallows Eve, I was born on sweet baby Jesus' birthday.

My parents like to call me their Christmas miracle. They'd been trying for years to get pregnant before they were blessed with me, and then I came on Christmas like the present they'd always wanted.

Suffice it to say I'm an only child, and my parents dote on me. I love my mom and dad, and I've never been starved for affection or anything, but my parents are older, which means that they have some old-school ways of thinking too.

I huff as I high-tail it down to the mall, cursing traffic along the way. I'm cursing myself for getting too caught up and being irresponsible yet again. I always do this. Mom swears I'll be late to my own funeral, and I'm begrudgingly starting to think that she's right. It doesn't seem to matter how early I get dressed or how much I try to plan ahead. I'm always running late.

I try to reason with myself, though. It's not like I'll get fired or anything. This is charity work, something I volunteered for and that my parents think is a waste of time, but it's something I really want to do.

If my parents had their way, I'd never work a day in my life or do anything but sit around the mansion and look pretty.

But I get bored with nothing to do, and I love children. I think that's what I love the most about Christmas—all the happiness of children. Growing up without any brothers or sisters, I was often lonely and always wished I'd had another kid around to play with. Sure, Mom and Dad took me to their friends' houses, but all their kids were usually several years older than me, so I was kind of too little to really make lasting friendships with any of them. I was always the little tag-along kid who got in the way of what the older kids wanted to do.

Plus, I hate staying cooped in the house, and it's not like I need any more money or anything, so I volunteer down at the children's hospital as much as I can—another activity that my parents don't necessarily approve of, though they admit that it's an "admirable pastime."

They don't realize it's more than just a pastime for me, though. I want to make a difference, and I love seeing the kids' faces light up when they get a visitor, especially the ones who are only children like me and incredibly lonely. I play silly games with them and do whatever I can to cheer them up.

And I love every minute of it, even if it is heartbreaking to see them so sick.

The hospital is where I learned about this Christmas gig down at the mall. I'm all dressed up as an elf to be Santa's helper as kids sit on his lap and tell him all their Christmas wishes before getting their pictures taken with him. I'll be directing the line and giving out toys to every kid who shows up.

Though it was supposed to be a paying gig, I wanted to do it so bad, I made sure I got picked by promptly telling the hiring manager that I'd do it for free and that I'd donate toys to be passed out to all the kids.

His eyes had about bugged out of his head at my offer, and I'd been hired on the spot. No doubt he thought I was some special kind of crazy, but who cares, right? I'll be doing what I love and helping kids.

Of course, I didn't tell my parents where this was all happening at. I didn't exactly lie to them. I told them what I was doing. I just didn't disclose the location. They'd lose their shit if they knew I was working down at the mall, which they thought was in a dangerous location.

They worry too much, though. I'll be in a big building with tons of people about. It's Christmastime, and families will be shopping and bringing their kids by to get their photos taken with Santa.

It's going to be a blast.

Nick

I look down at the red suit lined with white fur in disgust. I can't believe I'm wearing this shit, but a job is a job, and they're scarce enough to come by for felons like me. I'm lucky as hell I was even hired to do this considering my felony status and how I'll be in close contact with kids.

Not that I was locked up for anything so heinous as harming children. My blood boils at just the thought of the type of scum that would do something like that.

No, I did time for protecting my dumb ass idiot of a brother. Him and all his hare-brained ideas of get-rich-quick-schemes. The ungrateful little brat hasn't even had the decency to show his face to me since I got locked up—much less since I've gotten out, and for good reason.

He knows I owe him an ass beating for the past two years I spent in prison for a crime he committed—not me. I swooped in to save the day and talk some sense into his fool head and got caught in the crossfire—as in I'm the one who took the fall for everything when the cops showed up and the shit hit the fan.

Sure, I could have saved my ass and ratted my brother out, but if there's one thing I learned from growing up in the Bronx, it's that you don't rat on anyone, especially family. Even if you get pegged for some shit you're innocent of, you keep your goddamned mouth shut.

It's a code I've been proud to live by all my life, and I still don't regret not breaking it. I might have lost two years of my life, but I still have my honor.

That doesn't mean I'm not holding one hell of a grudge, though.

And I suspect my little bro knows that if his

continual absence and the fact that I haven't been able to locate him are any indication.

He's been living his life free and clear knowing damn well I've been sitting in a jail cell that had his name on it.

Now, I'm the one branded a felon, scraping by to make ends meet, ostracized from society.

It probably doesn't help that I'm a big mother-fucker. I was big before I went into the pen, towering over most other men at six-foot-five, but now I'm bulky and rippling with muscles too. There really isn't shit else to do in the pen other than exercise, and I had to do something to keep myself from going crazy.

I put the itchy ass white, curly beard on and slap the damn Santa cap on my head, but that's as far as I'm going. I'm not stuffing this suit with stuffing to try to make myself look like some over-weight, jolly fucker who eats too many cookies.

The man who hired me looks like he's about to protest when I fling the stuffing to the side, but one look at my glare and he wisely decides to keep his mouth shut.

"Your assistant should be here any minute," he says as he glances down at his watch with a frown.

I just nod, completely disinterested. I'd known there was going to have to be someone to play

Santa's helper. I just wish she would show up so we can get this show on the road and I can get this day over with and cash my paycheck before I move on to the next gig.

I don't know why, but in my mind, I assumed it would be some middle-aged woman dressed up as an elf for this effort, some kindly woman who loved children and maybe was down on her luck and scraping by to make ends meet herself.

That's why when this bubbly, young bombshell comes rushing into the mall and over to where Dave, the hiring manager, and I are standing, I'm frozen still with shock.

Tall for a girl, her golden skin almost seems to glow with purity under the natural sunlight that's flooding in through the domed skylight of the mall. Her platinum blonde hair is long and stick straight, coming down to rest right down below her slender waist.

I swallow as my eyes sweep hungrily over the rest of her. She's wearing little red tights that leave nothing to the imagination and a short green elvish dress that shows off her subtle curves. A little elf hat is cocked prettily on the top of her head.

But what has my heart suddenly hammering too loudly in my head are the big green eyes that she turns up to me as she rushes over. They're green as emeralds and just as sparkling. She beams up at me, a full, perfect, white smile. "Hey, Santa! Sorry to keep you waiting. Ugh, I got stuck in traffic." She's a flurry of activity, talking animatedly while she gestures with her hands and smiles enthusiastically at Dave.

I feel a rush of completely insane jealousy rise up within me when she turns those eyes and that smile onto the other man. I only want her looking at me that way. A growl bubbles up in my throat. I'm confused and irritated by my reaction to this girl who doesn't look a day over eighteen. Fuck, she looks like she should be in line to sit on my knee and tell me what she wants for Christmas. You can bet your ass I'd do anything within my power to give it to her too. She might be dressed up like an elf, but she looks more like an angel sent down from heaven.

I feel my cock stiffen within my pants at that thought and take a deep breath to try to calm myself. For fuck's sake.

My eyes zone in on her ruby red lips that are glistening with gloss. They remind me of ripe cherries, and I just know if I tasted them, that's exactly what the fuck she would taste like.

"How old are you?" I bark at her, my voice coming out much more roughly than I intend it to.

Her eyes flick back up to me as a little furrow forms in her brow. "Um, twenty-one, but why does that matter to you, Santa?" She answers me sassily with a little toss of her head before she counters back at me, "How old are *you*?"

I'm only twenty-eight, but I don't tell her that. I can't believe I'm only seven years older than her. I swear to God, the girl doesn't even look legal, but for some reason, I'm immensely relieved that she is.

"My name's Nick," I tell her. "Not fucking Santa." I can't stop the scowl that takes over my face. I meet the most beautiful creature I've ever laid eyes on and here I am wearing this ridiculous fucking Santa costume. I'm fuming with frustration and feel like an idiot.

A wide grin breaks across her face. "Really? Your name is really Nick, and you're playing Santa? Oh, this is priceless. Let me guess. Nick is short for Nicholas?"

I scowl at her. I realize she's making fun of me, but I'm so enamored by her smile, I don't even really give a shit. I'll let her laugh at me all day if it means I get to see that beautiful smile and that twinkle in her eyes.

I wipe the scowl off my face and feel my lips twitch. Her bright happiness and laugher are infectious. I could bask in her glow all day. "What's your name, doll?"

Do I imagine the blush that stains her pretty cheeks before she answers back with a cute little toss of her head? "Jenny."

"Jenny," I try her name out for size. "Short for Jennifer, I presume?" I ask her, raising an eyebrow of my own.

She frowns and fiddles with a piece of her hair as she answers, "Well, yes, but no one calls me *Jennifer* except my mom, and that's only when I'm in trouble or something."

"Oh, I bet you're trouble, Jennifer," I tell her as I take a step toward her. Her scent, something like cinnamon and apples, teases my nostrils, and I feel my blood surging within my veins.

Her face colors and her breath hitches, but she stands her ground and looks up at me as she firmly corrects me, "Jenny." Then she goes on with a shrug, "Well, I'm certainly no saint." She looks back up at me with mischievous eyes. "Not like you, Saint Nick."

I love the teasing glint sparkling in her green depths. I could engage in this playful banter with her all day.

"Make no mistake, *Jennifer*," I stress every

syllable of her name, loving the way it rolls off my tongue. "I am no saint. Far from it."

Before she has a chance to toss back what I'm sure would be another witty retort, Dave clears his throat beside us before announcing that we should get into position. The booth is set to open soon.

"After you," I gesture for her to walk ahead of me, now even more anxious for this day to be over with so we'll be off the clock and I can learn more about this little firecracker who's going to be my helper all day.